GLADIATOR BOY
vs
THE LIVING DEAD

Win an exclusive
Gladiator Boy T-shirt and goody bag!

Use the special code below to decode the sentence, then send it in to us.
Each month we will draw one winner to receive a Gladiator Boy T-shirt
and goody bag.

Send your entry on a postcard to:
GLADIATOR BOY: ESCAPE FROM THE EAST COMPETITION,
Hodder Children's Books, 338 Euston Road, London NW1 3BH

Only one entry per child.
Final Draw: 31 December 2010

You can also enter this competition via the Gladiator Boy website

WWW.GLADIATORBOY.COM

GLADIATOR BOY

VS

THE LIVING DEAD

DAVID GRIMSTONE

Hodder
Children's
Books

A division of Hachette Children's Books

A Catalogue record for this book is available from
the British Library

ISBN: 978 0 340 98927 2

Typeset by Tony Fleetwood

Printed and bound in the UK by CPI Bookmarque, Croydon, CR0 4TD

The paper and board used in this paperback by Hodder Children's Books
are natural recyclable products made from wood grown in
sustainable forests. The manufacturing processes conform to
the environmental regulations of the country of origin.

Hodder Children's Books
a division of Hachette Children's Books
338 Euston Road, London NW1 3BH
An Hachette UK company

www.hachette.co.uk

For Chris Brown, for being ammmmezin!

This new series is dedicated to Leilani Sparrow,
who has worked tirelessly with Gladiator Boy
since his arrival. Thanks also to Anne McNeil,
who has stood in my corner since day one.

HOW MANY

GLADIATOR BOY

BOOKS DO YOU HAVE?

DAVID GRIMSTONE

GLADIATOR BOY

A HERO'S QUEST

DAVID GRIMSTONE

GLADIATOR BOY

FREE GLADIATOR GAME INSIDE

ESCAPE FROM EVIL

DAVID GRIMSTONE

GLADIATOR BOY

STOWAWAY SLAVES

DAVID GRIMSTONE

GLADIATOR BOY

THE REBELS' ASSAULT

DAVID GRIMSTONE

GLADIATOR BOY

FREE GLADIATOR GAME INSIDE

RESCUE MISSION

DAVID GRIMSTONE

GLADIATOR BOY

FREE GLADIATOR GAME INSIDE

THE BLADE OF FIRE

GLADIATOR BOY VS THE LIVING DEAD

DAVID GRIMSTONE

GLADIATOR BOY VS THE RAGING TORRENT

FREE GAMES AND MODEL INSIDE

DAVID GRIMSTONE

GLADIATOR BOY VS THE THREE NINJAS

FREE GAMES AND MODEL INSIDE

DAVID GRIMSTONE

GLADIATOR BOY VS THE INSANE FURY

DAVID GRIMSTONE

GLADIATOR BOY VS THE WHITE SNAKE

THE WHITE SNAKE

FREE GAMES AND MODEL INSIDE

DAVID GRIMSTONE

GLADIATOR BOY VS THE GOLEM ARMY

FREE GAMES AND MODEL INSIDE

DAVID GRIMSTONE

CHINA

PREVIOUSLY IN GLADIATOR BOY

Captured by the evil overlord Slavious Doom, Decimus Rex is taken to the terrifying Arena Primus and entered into a series of brutal trials in order to earn his freedom. During the trials, Decimus makes five close friends – Gladius, Olu, Teo, Ruma, and Argon.

As the trials narrow down the competition and it becomes clear that the slaves will soon have to face each other, Decimus and Olu escape, experiencing a number of incredible adventures as they attempt to evade the forces of Slavious Doom. Sadly, these end with the slaves being recaptured in a cunning trap that also leads to the death of Teo, the smallest and weakest of the group.

It seems that Doom has secret plans for Decimus Rex and has merely been testing him in order to prepare him for a more important quest. Decimus is told that if he ever wishes to see his friends again, he must enter into the deadly maze beneath the arena and find the legendary Blade of Fire.

Unfortunately for Doom, things don't quite go to plan. Decimus rescues his friends, but the sword is destroyed, resulting in the complete collapse of the arena. Doom is left thwarted and totally furious, and the slaves return to their lives as free boys . . .

CHAPTER
I

THE FIVE

MAPS

It was deserted in the Great Garden, as the sweltering afternoon sun had forced even the most lazy inhabitants of the neighbouring towns to stay inside. Only the guards still patrolled the borders, commanded to protect the site by the emperor himself. It had once been home to an ancient temple, and was therefore considered to be of great importance to the empire.

Decimux Rex peered through the bushes, and muttered a curse under his breath. One or two guards would have been easy enough to deal with . . . but he'd counted at least five from his hiding place, not to mention the two near him at the gate. He wondered briefly if the others were here, but quickly dismissed the thought as wishful thinking . . .

Decimus was still crouched down, pondering his next move, when a whirring sound became audible in the distance, rising steadily in pitch as it drew closer.

Wwhhoomm.

Wwwhhhooommm.

Wwwwwhhhhhoooooooommmmmmmm.

Decimus almost gasped as an iron ball flew past the bush he was concealed in, moving through the air so fast that it was a mere blur to the two armoured guards on sentry duty by the gate. Unfortunately, the ball failed to strike either of them and instead hit the iron bars of the gate with an almighty clatter.

Decimus seized upon the distraction, and immediately snatched up a rock from the hard-packed ground beside the bush, hurling the missile with such deadly accuracy that it dropped the taller guard where he stood.

His companion immediately leapt into action, but Decimus still had the advantage of surprise. He waited for the second guard to pass the bush before exploding from the foliage and driving his fist hard into the man's unprotected jaw. The guard staggered back and reached for his sword, but was caught with two more blows before he could raise the weapon to strike.

Decimus moved faster than lightning, leaping around the guard and driving a boot into the crease at the back of his left knee. The man folded over, and Decimus knocked him out with a single punch.

Silence reigned at the gates, with only Decimus's laboured breath to disturb it. Thankfully, he reflected, the noise had not been enough to alert the guard patrols inside the garden: otherwise, they would have been piling on top of him already. Maybe the gods *were* still watching over him. He peered into the bushes from where the iron ball had come.

'Gladius?' he called, staring at a thick clump of furze. 'Come out of there! I know it's you; I'd recognize your useless throwing anywhere. That ball was way off.'

'Rubbish,' said a familiar voice, and Gladius wrestled his way out of the bush. 'If he hadn't moved at the last minute, it would have got him square in the chest. And anyway it was a perfect distraction for you.'

'Fair enough,' Decimus smiled, and greeted his old friend with a hug. 'Long time, no see. I take it you're here for the same reason I am?'

A look of sudden worry flashed across Gladius's big, honest face. 'Well, I got a message from Teo, if that's what you mean. You too?'

Decimus nodded, but his eyes narrowed to slits.

'If we both got them,' he muttered, 'you can bet the others did, too. They're probably on their way as we speak.' The young gladiator peered around him. 'We need to clear the garden – there's loads of guards on duty, and we don't want to end up totally surrounded.'

Gladius cracked his knuckles, and whistled between his teeth.

'I'm ready if y—' he began, but he was unable to finish. An enormous guard charged out from inside the garden gates and slammed into the pair like a rogue cannonball.

Decimus dodged left at the last moment, but Gladius took the full force of the assault and was cast aside like a bundle of rags.

Decimus took several leaps back in order to see exactly what he was dealing with. The guard was a monster, plain and simple; grotesquely overweight and covered in plates of patchy armour that failed to conceal the terrible odour created by the man's sweating flesh.

The hulking brute fought to regain his balance after the charge, then changed direction and came for Decimus in another pitched assault.

There wasn't enough space to avoid the monster twice, so Decimus braced himself for the collision and dug his feet into the dusty soil. It didn't achieve much as he was quickly thrust off his feet and driven hard against the garden wall. He managed to catch his breath and used all his strength to spring away from the wall once more, just as the enormous guard leapt forward to crush him. There was a heavy thud as flesh met stone, but the brute was only dazed. Crouching low, Decimus drove a fist into the back of the man's knee, and followed it up with an elbow to the spine; unfortunately, his second blow met one of the patchy sheets of armour, and he let out a strangled cry of pain.

Luckily, the attack was enough to catch the guard off balance and, as he staggered around to find his foe once again, Gladius powered into him. This time, the former slave had the advantage of the charge . . . and his weight lent him enough strength to take the big guard off his feet. Decimus didn't waste a second; still grimacing with pain, he scrambled on top of the prone giant and glanced a carefully aimed punch off the man's chin. There was a muffled grunt, and the big guard went out, cold.

'Good going,' Gladius panted, leaning over and resting both hands on his knees.

Decimus nodded, but gave his friend a doubtful look. 'I hope there aren't too many more like *him* in the garden,' he said. 'I'm not sure I could fight that monster twice.'

At the other end of the garden, three burly sentries were playing a game that involved rolling several small stones along the ground in an attempt to hit a larger one. But the game was interrupted when a scrawny, weathered-looking youth stepped on to the middle of the path.

'Who's got the brain?' said Ruma, kicking several stones aside as the guards all gasped in astonishment. 'Only, I've been watching you idiots from the bushes and I reckon there MUST be only *one* actual brain between the three of you – that is if you're lucky.'

The three men looked at one another, dropped their rocks and rushed forward. As they did, the undergrowth on either side of them parted, and Olu and Argon ploughed into the men and began raining blows on them with a war-like battle cry.

Argon had muscled up, considerably; he was almost twice the size he'd been during his days in the arena, and his arms were like two blocks of iron. Olu was still slender, but fought with great skill: he'd spent a long time training since he and the others had parted company.

Ruma hadn't changed at *all*. The wiry Etrurian was as deadly as ever: every dodge was successful, every blow on target.

In practically no time at all, the guards lay in an awkward heap ... and the boys stood around

the path, admiring their handiwork. It was Ruma who spoke first.

'We need to get to the centre of the garden,' he muttered, carefully prodding one guard with the edge of his foot and then peering along the path. 'Decimus and Gladius are probably there, already . . . though I can't see anyone standing around the Head Stone, yet . . .'

Olu flashed him a knowing smile. 'That doesn't mean they're not there,' he muttered. 'You wouldn't see Decimus unless he wanted you to.'

The Head Stone had been the centrepiece of the Great Garden for as long as anyone could remember. It was a large, rectangular block of granite, supported at each end by two smaller rocks. Some people thought it looked like a big stone table, but many suspected it had once served as a magical altar of some sort.

As Ruma, Olu and Argon approached the little hill on which the Head Stone stood, they noticed that a group of guards lay sprawled around the clearing; all of them seemed to be unconscious. There was no sign of Decimus or Gladius.

'They've been here,' Ruma said, pointing at the prone guards. 'No doubt about that.'

Olu and Argon nodded in agreement, but almost jumped out of their skin when Decimus dropped from a tree beside the path and slapped them on their shoulders.

'I could've taken you both out of the picture then,' he chuckled. 'It's a good job Gladius and I got rid of the rest of the guards.' He grinned at the group. 'I see you've beefed up a bit, Argon. It's good to see you again.'

'Yeah, yeah,' said Ruma, irritably. 'We're *all* happy to see each other again. But let's be honest, Decimus, none of us is here by choice. I assume we all got the same message, and are here to find out if—'

Decimus raised a hand to stop his friend talking.

'Hang on a minute, Ruma. I don't think we should take anything for granted. My message was delivered by a hooded crow . . . and you don't see many of them about. They're trained to serve one master, and I never remember Teo having a particular skill with crows.'

'Teo is *dead*,' Argon interrupted. 'We saw him hanged, remember? People who are dead do not write messages. Am I the only one with any sense here?'

'The whole thing is strange,' Olu agreed. 'We're being set up . . . probably by Slavious Doom. It's a trap, and an obvious one at that.'

'Doom hasn't come after us in nearly a *year*,' Gladius reminded them. 'Not since Arena Primus collapsed.'

Ruma shrugged. 'Maybe he realized he was lucky to come out of that place alive, and decided to forget about us?'

'Never,' said Decimus, sternly. 'Doom will never let us go. He's just playing it carefully, this time, laying a trap rather than sending guards to bring us in . . . he gets pleasure from setting traps, we *know* that. But even if I would willingly stake my life on it being a trap, we simply can't afford to ignore it. If – by some *miracle* – Teo *did* survive the noose . . . and we did nothing to help him . . .'

He reached into his pocket and produced a roll of parchment. 'My message says: Decimus, I need your help. I have already sent for the others. Please come to the Head Stone in the Great Garden. For the sake of our friendship, don't let me down. Teo.'

'It's as I said before,' Ruma muttered. 'We all got the same message.'

'Yes,' said Gladius, testily. 'But did we all get the same map?'

The former slave produced his own

parchment, unfurled the message and then turned it over so that the reverse side was on display. A single crooked line ran over the surface, with several place names dotted here and there along the line.

The others all looked at the revelation, quickly bringing out their own messages in order to study them. Each one was different.

'I can't believe I didn't see this,' Decimus snapped, making his way to the Head Stone and spreading his map out with the flat of his hands. The others quickly joined him.

'This is the entire eastern coastline,' Olu pointed out, piecing his own parchment together with those from his friends. 'I don't see anything special about it, though ...'

'Me neither,' Argon admitted. 'It can't be

anything to do with the places that are marked –
they're all just towns and villages.'

'Wait!' Decimus shouted suddenly, stepping
back from the maps. 'We must have been called
here, to this place, for a reason – it has to be
something to do with the Head Stone.'

Gladius frowned slightly, then began to move
his own parchment to the edge of the stone.
After a few seconds, his eyes lit up.

'Put them all in the middle!' he shouted.

'What?' Ruma barked back. 'Why? What
good—'

'Just do it!'

The group quickly rearranged their maps so
that they fitted together, but this time they
positioned the five tattered scraps in a rough
circle at the centre of the Head Stone. The

prominent engraving of a tiny shield on the
surface of the stone sat perfectly in the middle.

'That's it!' said Decimus, pointing at the
shield amid the parchment jigsaw. 'That's where
we need to go. If that was marked on a map,
where would it be?'

Olu, Argon and Ruma all looked momentarily puzzled; only Gladius was smiling.

'It's the Slaveyard,' he said, quietly at first.

'Say that again?'

'The Slaveyard,' Gladius repeated. 'It's a mass graveyard for slaves. It's maintained by the empire in an effort to make it look like they actually care for their servants . . . in death, at least.' He turned to Decimus, his eyebrows creased. 'You think that's where we need to go?'

'Definitely,' said the young gladiator, his voice dropping almost to the level of a snarl. 'It's the place where Doom's men had Teo buried . . . after they *murdered* him at Suvius Tower.'

CHAPTER
II

THE
SLAVEYARD

I t was midnight, and a full moon bathed the valley in a pale, eerie light. Unusually for this part of outer Brindisium, it was very cold ... and a shifting mist settled on the land.

Although the valley walls were rough and jagged, the land they encased was completely flat. It would have been the perfect spot for an arena, or even a large jail, but it hadn't been used for either purpose. Instead, it contained the infamous Slaveyard: three square miles of crudely fashioned stones and low burial mounds, all laid out in long, meandering lines.

Wandering between these grim avenues, just visible as odd shapes in the distance, were the keepers. It had long been rumoured that the keepers were originally hired slaves who'd been deformed in the arena; either through ferocious combat or encounters with various wild animals. Some of them were missing limbs, several were badly mauled and a few were too grotesque for words. However, the thing that made the keepers legendary was not their appearance; it was their dedication. These wretched victims of human cruelty watched over the dead with a determination bordering on insanity. Free men were forbidden to enter the Slaveyard; it was a place of regret, anger and despair ... and a place where slaves could finally rest in peace. The keepers guarded every inch of the yard with all their might – getting in without confrontation would be next to impossible.

'We're *not* harming the keepers,' Decimus

growled, peering down at the shapes in the Slaveyard. 'I don't care what we're trying to do, here: we'll do it *without* a fight.'

'You're not serious?' Argon snapped. 'The second we set foot on that ground, we'll be attacked!'

'He's right,' Ruma echoed. 'They're slow-moving, but there's no way we can get to Teo's grave *and* work out what we're looking for in the time it will take them to catch up with us.'

'Er ... I have an idea,' said Olu.

'Me too,' Gladius muttered. 'I wonder if we're thinking the same thing?'

They both turned to look at Argon.

Decimus and Ruma followed their gaze, but were as baffled as the Gaul.

'Did I miss something?' Argon asked,

uncomfortably aware of the attention. 'Why is everyone staring at me all of a sudden?'

'You're strong,' Olu said, simply. 'By the look of you, I reckon you're easily the strongest of us all.'

'I agree,' added Ruma. 'You could probably lift an elephant with those muscles.'

'You could certainly lift one of those marker stones,' said Olu. 'Which, I think, is what both Gladius and I had in mind.'

'Exactly,' Gladius nodded, and pointed towards one corner of the Slaveyard. 'If you go down *that* side of the valley, the trees will give you cover. When you get to the edge of the yard, you can run out, grab one of the smaller stones . . . and make off with it.'

Argon stared from Gladius to Olu, and back

again with a look of irritation on his face.

'Are you two crazy?' he snapped. 'Run where, exactly?'

'It doesn't matter,' said Decimus, beginning to understand the strategy. 'As long as you keep running circles around the keepers.'

Argon thought for a moment, and then rolled his eyes.

'So you want me to snatch a *sacred* stone marking the death of some poor slave and *dash* off with it so all of the keepers come after me?'

'Yes, while we all make for Teo's grave.'

'What about disturbing a sacred site? Have you lot suddenly lost all sense of respect or something? Apart from that, it's probably going to wake a restless spirit. We'll end up—'

'There's no such thing as ghosts,' Decimus

said, his face set in a grimace. 'And we don't have a choice; if there was any other way, we would do it . . . but there isn't. I'd rather disturb the peace of the dead than risk killing one of the living. Now, are we doing this or not?'

Argon hurried from the last line of trees and half ran, half staggered towards the edge of the Slaveyard. He'd opted to run in a strangely awkward manner so that the keepers might think he was one of them and not an intruder from the outside. The plan certainly seemed to be working, and it was only when he stooped to unearth one of the stones that he began to draw attention from the watchful eyes of the

Slaveyard's terrifying caretakers.

A large, one-armed man with scorched flesh, and a hefty scar where his right eye should have been, suddenly glanced in Argon's direction . . . and began to lope towards him. As he ran, he released a strangled cry, which in turn alerted several others that a stranger was present in the Slaveyard. To the surprise of the boys, who were still watching from the opposite end of the valley, the entire army of keepers began to run, stagger, crawl and in some cases even drag themselves towards Argon. It was almost instinctive; despite the mist, they all moved together in the same direction.

The Gaul, however, was putting in a powerful performance. He'd managed to wrestle a medium-sized marker stone from the ground and was heaving it on to his shoulder. As the

first of the keepers approached, he moved into a

slow jog and quickly began to pick up pace as

several twisted cries pierced the silence of the

Slaveyard.

Being careful not to sprint out of view,

Argon maintained a steady run,

leading the keepers around the

edge of the yard and off towards the side of the valley path.

Far behind them, the remaining boys entered the opposite end of the yard. Almost immediately, they divided up: Argon and Olu went east, while Decimus and Gladius headed west. The search was on.

'Some of these marker stones are faded!' Argon whispered. 'How are we supposed to find Teo's grave in this maze?'

'Teo's grave is hardly likely to be faded,' said Olu, reasonably. 'He's not been dead two years: the markings should still be readable.'

They moved between the stones, stopping briefly at each one to try to determine exactly how the lines were ordered.

'These are practically *all* ancient,' Olu

continued. 'I think we're in the wrong part
of the yard.'

Decimus stopped at a marker and crouched
beside it. Then he looked up again, squinting to
find Gladius in the misty gloom.

'Hey! Psst! Gladius!' he called, trying to keep
his voice as hushed as possible. 'You there?'

'Yes, *I* am! Where did you go when we first
divided up? I was calling but you didn't answer!'

'I saw something we might need ... and I
picked it up.'

'What is it?'

'Never mind that! Let's get on with the
search. This line of graves is three years old!

What about yours?'

'Er . . . hang on,' Gladius replied. 'I'm trying to see whether . . . whoah . . . I think these are *very* recent. There's one here from last month!'

Decimus squinted into the mist. 'How many lines over are you?'

'Uh . . . two, I think.'

'Then it must be the line between us! Come on; we'll meet in the middle!'

The two slaves dashed along the new avenue, taking a little more time with each stone in an effort not to miss a single marker.

'Tolverto!' Gladius whispered. 'Dead for one year and two months!'

'Erano!' Decimus called back. 'One year, four months.'

'Thenos! One year, five months!'

'Irin! One year, seven months!'

'It's Teo, Decimus! I've found him! It says one year, eight months – er – that has to be it, right?'

There was a second of silence.

'OK! Stay there,' Decimus shouted. 'I'll go get the others!'

Argon was running out of steam.

He'd carried the heavy stone on his shoulder for several minutes, but now the weight combined with the uphill run to put incredible pressure on the former slave.

To make matters worse, the keepers had proved more determined pursuers than even Olu had suspected, and if anything were gaining on him enough to be a dangerous threat. If they caught him, he wouldn't be able to fight them all off . . .

Without pausing to consider an alternative course of action, Argon suddenly dumped the stone off his

shoulder and used the last reserves of his
energy to put on a last-second sprint.

He dashed away up the hill and along the
high side to check that the keepers weren't still
following him. Mercifully, they had gathered
around the stone and were attempting to raise it
once more.

They would return the marker to its rightful place before searching the valley for him.

The group gathered around Teo's grave, their heads bowed in respectful silence. It was Decimus that broke the reverie.

'I'm sorry about this, Teo, old friend,' he muttered and, to the astonishment of the others, produced a rough spade from behind his back and began to dig the dirt in front of the stone.

'What are you doing?' Gladius gasped, dumbfounded.

'Where did you get that from?' said Ruma and Olu, together.

Decimus ignored both questions and
continued to dig frantically, employing
the shovel to hurl great mounds of dirt
up on either side of him.

The others merely looked on, aghast.

'You can stare all you like,' said Decimus,
defiantly. 'The message brought us to this place,
and considering the stone consists of nothing
except a name and a date, what we're supposed
to uncover *must* be in the grave itself – trap or no
trap. So I'm digging.'

'We'd better help,' Olu remarked, leaping
into the hole beside his friend and scooping
out handfuls of dusty earth. Ruma quickly
joined them.

'I'll keep watch,' said Gladius, doubtfully. He
looked out over the Slaveyard, and noticed that

the swirling mist was beginning to clear.

'Any sign of Argon?' asked Olu, flinging another scoop of soil out of the hole.

Gladius shook his head. 'None ... but I *can* see the keepers. They're coming back down the valley, and they have the marker stone with them.'

'Great,' Ruma muttered. 'If we don't get a move on, we'll—'

THUNK.

'What was that?'

Decimus drove the shovel down again.

THUNK.

THUNK.

There was no doubt: the shovel had hit wood.

As the three friends scrambled at the dirt, Gladius took a generous step *away* from the graveside. 'Is that ... Teo?' he asked, nervously.

'No.' Decimus grunted. 'Slaves don't get the luxury of a coffin: this is something else.'

He crouched down and helped Olu and Ruma to brush the last of the dirt from the surface of the box, and

together they lifted it out of the grave.

It wasn't much bigger than the box Gladius used at home for his sandals. Ruma lifted it out with ease, and deposited it on the ground at Gladius's feet. Then he and Olu climbed out. Only Decimus remained in the grave.

'We're not opening it here, are we?' Gladius said, pointing at the distant keepers, who had repositioned the stolen marker and were now heading back between the stones.

'No,' said Decimus, wearily. 'You three take that box and get out of here; I'll meet you on the edge of the valley.'

Gladius picked up the box, and handed it to Olu, but Ruma was staring down at Decimus with vague puzzlement.

'What are you doing now?' asked the Etrurian. 'Shouldn't we *all* be getting out of this place right *now?*'

Decimus shook his head, determinedly.

'Not until I've gone down further – if Teo's in here, we're definitely walking into a very dangerous trap.'

Ruma frowned. 'And what if he isn't?'

'If he *isn't* . . . well, I don't even want to think about that possibility.'

CHAPTER III

THE SECRET REVEALED

everal miles from the Slaveyard, Gladius dropped to his knees and promptly folded over, collapsing into the dirt.

Olu came to a halt shortly afterwards, bending slightly to support himself as he puffed out a great lungful of air.

Ruma was still running, however, and they had to call him back.

'I'm not moving another inch,' Gladius spat, from the ground. 'Can't we just open the stupid box *here*?'

'We probably shouldn't go on anyway,' said Olu, doubtfully. 'Decimus and Argon will *never* catch up if we put another mile between us and that Slaveyard.'

'What if the keepers got hold of them?' said Ruma, arriving beside them: the scrawny Etrurian wasn't even out of breath.

'They didn't,' said a voice.

Argon stepped on to the path. He looked weathered and weary, and his muscles were glistening with sweat.

'Decimus got away before they reached him.

He threw down the shovel and ran off south. I don't doubt he'll be here in a few—'

Argon stopped speaking, a worried look on his face. The others, all in various stages of exhaustion, turned to see what he was staring at.

Decimus was walking determinedly up the path. This should have been a considerable relief to the group, but the young gladiator's expression was one of furious and boiling anger.

Without so much as a word to the others, Decimus marched straight up to Olu, snatched the box out of his friend's arms and raised it over his head.

'Wait!'

Gladius scrambled to his feet, and Olu flung out his arms in panic. Ruma and Argon were too stunned to move.

'Decimus!'

'What's happened?'

'What are you doing?'

Decimus raised the box over his head and brought it down on to the path with all his might. The wood splintered, but the box didn't break entirely. Still ignoring the questions and shocked expressions from the rest of the group, Decimus snatched up the weakened box and repeated the action. This time, he hurled it at the ground with such force that it fell apart completely.

Inside was a scroll of parchment wrapped around some sort of object.

Decimus reached down for it.

'I'm angry,' he said, glancing around at his gathered companions. 'Teo's body *isn't* in the grave. We *know* he's dead, so we just have to assume that Doom took his body as some sort of sick trap he's setting for us all. *This* thing, whatever it is, must be the first part of the puzzle.'

Decimus began to unfurl the scroll. As he did so, it became clear that the object he was holding was in fact a statue, crudely fashioned in the shape of a warrior but clearly made from gold.

'Is it solid?' Argon asked.

Decimus hefted the statue in his hand. 'It's

really, really heavy,' he said. 'Does anyone know what it is?'

The group muttered vaguely.

'It's not like any warrior I've ever seen,' Ruma admitted.

'Same here,' said Olu and Argon together.

Gladius, however, had his head on one side.

'There's *something* familiar about it,' said the big youth, who was generally considered to be more schooled than his friends. 'But I can't quite put my finger on it – what does the scroll say?'

Decimus looked down at the parchment in his other hand – in all the fuss over the golden statue, he'd almost forgotten about it.

Handing the warrior to Olu, he unrolled the script and read the message scrawled on it aloud:

Friends . . . need your help . . . pain . . . being held . . . dark place . . . prisoner . . . my own land . . . place I do not recognize . . . save me . . . the tower . . . I survive still . . .

Teo

'It's pathetic,' said Decimus, almost growling the words. 'Doom has had nearly two years to come up with a trap, and this is the best he can do . . . with all the resources and armoured thugs he must have working for him now? Apart from anything else, Teo couldn't write a message like this . . .'

'Maybe somebody else wrote it for him?' said Gladius, carefully. 'Somebody who wants to help us find him?'

'Like who?' said Olu, confused.

Decimus scrunched the scroll into a ball and tossed in on to the dusty ground. 'You're not serious?' he snapped. 'This is all *nonsense* and you idiots are falling for it!'

'What if it *isn't* nonsense?' said Ruma. 'What if he *did*, by some wonderful miracle, survive the hanging at Suvius Tower?'

'He didn't!' Decimus snapped. 'We all *saw* him lying there on the ground – we all saw him *dead*.'

'I don't care what we saw,' said Ruma suddenly. The scrawny Etrurian strode over to Decimus and looked him straight in the eye. 'While there's even the slightest element of doubt, the tiniest *chance* that Teo lives, well, I for one am going to try to help him.'

Ruma took the statue from Olu's unresisting hands and bent down to pick up the crushed scroll.

'Is anyone coming with me, or am I doing this alone?' he said. The look on his face dared them all to argue.

'I'm with you,' said Olu, moving to stand

beside the Etrurian.

'Goes without saying,' Gladius agreed, mooching over to the pair with a glum look on his face.

'If I *must*,' Argon spat, a resentful tone to his voice.

Decimus waited a few seconds, gritted his teeth defiantly, and then let out an exhausted sigh.

'Well, I'm not just going to stand idly by while you gullible fools walk straight into a trap,' he growled, folding his arms in exasperation. 'But it's Doom behind all this . . . *I'm* telling you.'

The old shack stood alone, occupying the crest of a steep hill that overlooked distant Tarentum. People tended to walk miles to avoid the shack, partly because the hill was so steep but mostly because the man who lived inside it was rumoured to be insane. In fact, on several occasions, the owner of the shack had been known to run outside in a screaming fit and attack passers-by.

Decimus and his companions didn't avoid the shack, however: in fact, they made straight for it.

'Who *is* this ... er ... *Sturgeus?*' Olu enquired. 'Can he really be trusted?'

'It's Sturgenus,' said Decimus, wearily. 'And I've already told you: he hates Slavious Doom *and* the empire. The problem is, he also hates everyone else. If we want his help, I'm afraid we're in for a fight . . . and he isn't a pushover.'

Argon suddenly stopped dead halfway up the hill. 'Is it really worth getting involved in *another* mad brawl just to get some information?' he hazarded. 'How do you actually know this man, anyway?'

'I don't,' Decimus admitted. 'My father met him when he was a scholar. He lived near us in Tarentum. He told me Sturgenus was the smartest person he ever met . . . I suppose he got too smart in the end, and went a bit – you know – insane.'

'How insane, exactly?' Gladius wondered aloud. 'I mean, are we talking slightly eccentric or a total lunatic?'

'Well, he hates visitors – I know that. Oh, and . . .'

The group continued towards the shack, but all eyes were on Decimus as he muttered some sort of inaudible answer under his breath.

'What was that?' Olu prompted.

Decimus rolled his eyes and reluctantly raised his voice.

'Look, don't get too excited about this,' he said, slowly. 'But, well, Sturgenus . . . he killed three guards. Now just shut up and let's pay him a visit . . . carefully.'

The shack was eerily quiet as Decimus raised a tentative hand and knocked sharply on the door.

'Sturgenus? Are you in?'

Silence.

'Sturgenus? My name is Decimus; I believe you knew my father, Fenzo?'

There was no reply, and the hilltop suddenly felt very isolated from the surrounding landscape.

Decimus knocked a third time, then signalled for Gladius, Olu and Argon to move around to the rear of the shack.

'Try to see inside,' he whispered. 'If he isn't here, we might have to wait for him.'

When they'd all disappeared from view, Decimus put a hand to the door and gently pushed it open.

Instinctively, Ruma crowded in behind.

The door creaked open. Inside, the shack was in total darkness. A sliver of moonlight raced across the floor as the door yawned wide, revealing a floor covered with thick, dusty scrolls and tattered parchments of all shapes and sizes. A bedroll was occupying a tiny corner of the room, but apart from that every available space was filled with some variety of scripture. Aside from the shifting shadows, nothing moved.

'Follow me,' Decimus whispered. 'Quietly.'

He took one step inside the shack.

Then another.

And another.

Finally, he relaxed – and Sturgenus dropped from the ceiling like a giant spider leaping from a concealed web.

The door to the shack exploded outwards, and Decimus flew through the opening like a dart, hitting the ground with such speed that he

actually skimmed along like a stone hurled over water. As he eventually slowed to a halt, he folded up and grabbed at his back with a pained cry.

There were several further screams from within, and Ruma staggered outside, clutching

a wound on the side of his head and moaning
very loudly.

As Gladius, Argon and Olu reappeared from
the back of the shack, Sturgenus exploded from
the doorway and ran straight towards them: the

deranged old man was carrying a battered chair-leg, waving it wildly over his head and screaming.

'Run!' Ruma screamed, wincing at the pain in his skull. 'He's completely mental!'

Gladius, Olu and Argon all leapt into action, but Decimus's voice echoed around them.

'Careful! He's got a weapon!'

All eyes turned to Sturgenus, who had seemingly exploded into a windmill of raging arms and legs.

Olu heeded Decimus's warning without time to spare, dodging aside half a second before the chair-leg whirred past. He took the near-miss as an opportunity to throw a punch of his own at the old man, but it was like hitting a strip of leather, and Sturgenus only cackled when the blow connected with his arm.

Argon tried a more direct method of combat, charging into the old man and using his improved strength to try to lift him off his feet. The plan worked, but was quickly thwarted when Sturgenus drove his head directly into the young gladiator's face. Argon released his grip and staggered back, tripping over Gladius, who had tried and failed to make his own grab for the crazy old man. They ended up as a mess of limbs, and neither one of them managed to get back to their feet.

Decimus came running up the hill once again, but this time he took a slight detour. Hurrying around the side of the hill, he snatched up two smallish rocks and promptly made for the door of the shack.

As he tried to pass Sturgenus, the old man snatched at his tunic and dragged him back, folding an arm around his neck in an effort to choke him. He might have succeeded in rendering the young gladiator unconscious had Ruma not recovered from his earlier wound and taken the opportunity to land a well-aimed blow to the small of his back.

Sturgenus yelped angrily and, relaxing his grip on Decimus's throat, rounded on the Etrurian with a strangled cry of murderous fury. Briefly forgotten, Decimus tightened his grip on the stones and crawled inside the shack.

Meanwhile, the battle was intensifying . . .

Never one to back away from a fight, Ruma made an unwise decision and decided to goad the dangerous lunatic who was stalking him.

'Come on!' he cried, backing away. 'This way, you crazy fool! See if you can catch me!'

He soon discovered the answer to that question, however, as he hadn't even turned on his heel before the old man managed to sprint across the path and snatch hold of him.

'What the—'

'STOP RIGHT THERE, STURGENUS!' The booming cry came from the shack, as shadows began to dance in the doorway. Decimus appeared from within. He was holding a piece of burning parchment aloft in one hand. '... OR YOUR PRECIOUS SCROLLS WILL BE TURNED TO ASH!'

A sudden silence settled on the scene, as a look of intense horror crept across the old man's face.

'N-n-no,' he said, nervously. 'N-n-not my p-p-precious s-s-scrolls!'

'We just want to talk to you,' said Decimus, still holding the flaming parchment above his head. 'A few moments of your time, and then we're gone. Do you understand what I say?'

Sturgenus growled under his breath, like some sort of wild dog, but he somehow managed to smile at the same time, putting Decimus in mind of a crazed jackal.

'I underst-st-stand,' he said. 'Go ins-s-side.'

He half sprang, half hobbled over to Decimus, and the others – battered, bruised and bleeding – followed after him.

CHAPTER IV

THE

SHIP

THIEVES

S turgenus walked, crab-like, to the middle of the room. Kicking a pile of scrolls aside, he cleared a small space and slumped down on to the floor. The others all gathered around him, but nobody sat too close: many of the boys were convinced the old man would go berserk again at any moment. At least the door had been left open for an easy escape route. A wash of moonlight illuminated the inside of the shack.

Only Decimus spoke to Sturgenus directly.

'We're trying to find a friend of ours,' said the young gladiator. 'We believe he's been . . . taken by Doom and his men.'

Sturgenus glowered at them all, but said nothing. Instead he looked down at the still burning parchment they had laid on the ground before him, and quickly stamped out the flames.

'Anyway,' Decimus continued, awkwardly, as Gladius passed him the crumpled scroll they'd found in Teo's grave, 'this is all we have to go on at the moment.'

The old man snatched the parchment, but went on glaring at the boys for some time before turning his attention to it. His watery, maniacal eyes scanned the lines of text. Then he threw the scroll back at them.

'Tells m-me n-n-nothing,' he spat. 'J-just a n-n-note full of n-n-nonsense.'

'That's what I thought,' the young gladiator admitted. 'What about this, though?'

At a nod from Decimus, the golden statue was brought forward. Gladius, who'd been carrying it, seemed very reluctant to hand the object over. He remained holding on to it for a few seconds after Decimus had taken hold of the statue's base. Finally, after a less than gentle tug from Decimus, Gladius released his grip and Decimus handed the statue to their resentful host.

The old man's eyes widened as soon as he saw it, and he greedily snatched the warrior and held it up to the moonlight.

'Can I k-k-keep it?' he enquired.

Before anyone could protest, Decimus held up a hand for quiet. Ignoring the sudden warning glares from Olu, Argon, Ruma and Gladius, he nodded in agreement.

'If you help us,' he said. 'You can take it as payment.'

'A golden statue!' Ruma yelled, suddenly. 'Tell me you're joking!'

'He'd better be,' Argon added, shooting Decimus an unpleasant grin. 'Or we'll need to have words outside.'

The young gladiator looked at them all in turn. His expression was resolute.

'Listen,' he began. 'Of course I'm not going to give this *valuable* warrior to Sturgenus for *nothing*. He's not getting it unless he tells us something that will help us to find Teo. If he doesn't, we'll just take it back and walk out of h—'

'Yelang,' said the old man, suddenly.

All attention turned to him.

'What was that?' prompted Olu.

Sturgenus sighed, and coughed a little. 'It's a Y-y-yelang w-warrior.'

'What is Yelang?' asked Decimus.

'Not what; *w-w-where.*'

Ruma frowned. 'OK . . . *where* is Yelang, then? Somewhere in China? I'm sure Teo was from—'

'Han Dynasty. S-s-southern Ch-ch-china.' Sturgenus turned the statue over in his hands. 'This s-s-statue was made in the W-w-winter Palace there. V-very r-r-rare. Very rare ind-d-deed. It m-must be worth a f-f-fort—'

Before Sturgenus could finish his sentence, Decimus leapt to his feet.

'Come on,' he said. 'We need to go now.'

Argon gawped at him.

'Go where, exactly? China's halfway across the world, remember? How are *we* going to get there?'

The young gladiator shrugged, as the boys all clambered to their feet.

'We find a ship,' he said, simply. 'We've done it before.'

Sensing that he no longer had their full attention, Sturgenus cradled the statue and crawled off towards his bedroll. In the morning, he'd try and sell it in Tarentum. Then he could buy a new home for himself: one with more room for his scrolls.

'I suppose we could find a ship,' Gladius was saying. 'But it isn't going to be easy. We might even have to—'

'NO!'

The sudden shout had come from Olu, who staggered to his feet and pointed directly at Decimus. 'We'll look for a ship, fine, agreed, but *this time*, Decimus, we'll find someone who'll agree to let us on board. We are *not* stowing away – not *again* – and definitely not for a journey halfway around the world.'

Decimus grinned, and the group wandered out of the shack, leaving Sturgenus to his new prize.

'We need to go back to Brindisium, but we can't hit the main docks there,' said Gladius, shaking his head. 'There'll be too many guards and I can't imagine finding a major ship willing to take us that far without a hefty amount of coinage.'

'So where *do* we find passage, if we can't go to the docks?' Ruma moaned.

'Further up the coast, there's a little-known mooring point' said Gladius, knowledgeably. 'Some of the less ... er ... confident captains put in there.'

Ostuni Bay was never busy.

This was, in the most part, because the Ostunians tended to keep their trades quiet. Several small vessels arrived in the bay each day, but usually one at a time and never for more than an hour on each occasion.

Currently, there was a single boat moored at the town's tiny jetty. It was more of an ageing tramp schooner than an ocean-faring ship, but it was nevertheless attracting the wrong kind of attention. The bay, known for its secrecy, had evidently been discovered.

A team of five men were making for the jetty; they didn't look like guards or soldiers, but they *did* seem very intent on reaching the boat at speed. The reason for this was quite simple: word had leaked out, and they'd heard about the cargo. There was only *one* boat due to arrive at this time on this day, and it carried valuable spices.

Halfway to the jetty, the five men broke into a determined run. Each one was armed with a sword, and moved with impressive agility.

The captain of the schooner, a man called Tonino, knew immediately that his cargo was in trouble. Aware that his trading partners weren't due for another hour, he was struggling with the mooring ropes even before the men had started to run, desperate to free his vessel from the jetty.

He wasn't going to make it in time.

'This place is practically deserted,' Decimus muttered, as he and the group stepped on to the winding path that led down into Ostuni Bay. 'The town looks abandoned and there's only *one* pathetic boat in the water.'

Gladius rolled his eyes and sighed. 'Didn't you lot listen to anything I told you on the way here?' he muttered. 'Firstly, the town *is* empty: that's why the secret traders use it. Secondly, one boat is all we need ... and the smaller, the better. We're hardly going to be able to convince a big-league captain to divert his ship to China, are we?'

There were various mutterings from the group, but they continued on the path.

'Now *that's* lucky timing,' said Olu, suddenly. 'They're unloading the cargo.'

Decimus relaxed slightly. 'At least we don't need to run,' he said. 'I think I've spent enough energy for one day.'

'That's odd,' said Argon, suddenly, squinting over towards the jetty.

'Mmm? What's odd?'

'Well, this whole place is deserted,' the Gaul went on, 'yet they're still running with those crates as if the entire army was after them.

What's the hurry?'

'Maybe they think *we're* the army?' Olu hazarded. 'Besides, they're only loading them on to that cart: they probably can't afford to hang around for long.'

'No,' said Ruma, suddenly. 'Something's wrong. None of those men look like sailors to me; they're in a rush because they're robbing the boat! I'd bet my life on it! Quick! Let's move! They won't see us coming if we're really fast . . .'

Without another word, Ruma hared off down the path as if he'd been possessed. Argon glanced at Decimus, and they both hurried after him. Gladius and Olu both made for the boat, instead.

The robbers had divided up and were now halfway through their raid. One had climbed aboard the cart and was preparing the horse to move. Three others were loading up the crates while the leader stayed on the boat in order to subdue the captain. It was all going *exactly* according to plan.

'Get a move on, will you?' the driver called back at his companions. 'We need to get going, here!'

'Boss is still on the boat,' said one of the men lifting in the last crate. 'Just a few more seconds.'

'Yeah, well, I don't think we should h—'

The driver was cut off in mid-sentence: Ruma cannoned into him with incredible force, an ambush that forced them both to the ground.

The horse reared up wildly as two of the loaders immediately dropped the crate they were carrying and went for their swords. Neither made it; Decimus and Argon were all over them in seconds.

The third loader immediately drew his own blade and stepped back, calling over his shoulder for the robber who'd stayed on the boat.

'Boss? Boss! We're under attack! Ambush! Ambush!'

A fifth man appeared from the cabin of the boat, and dashed towards the jetty. Leaping the prow, he put on a determined sprint ... and ran right into the waiting arms of Gladius and Olu.

The two former slaves had linked hands and formed a clothes-line that not only took the head robber completely by surprise, but also swept him off his feet like a tree branch taking a rider off a horse. He hit the jetty floor with a dull thud, and Gladius dropped on him with one elbow outstretched. While the man fought in vain to wrestle him off, Olu snatched his sword from its scabbard and carefully entered the boat.

'Hlllp!' came a muffled cry from the cabin. 'Hllllllp mmmmmeeee!'

Olu hurried over to the small hatchway, and wrenched it open. Inside was a short, bearded man tied up with several lengths of rope.

Argon wrenched one of the robbers off his feet and threw the stunned man against the side of the cart. Before he could recover, the young gladiator followed up with three swift punches that knocked the wind from him, and finished with a knee-lift that knocked the man out, cold. Unfortunately, before he could reach for the prone robber's sword, he suddenly felt a blade pressed underneath his throat.

'Get up,' said a soft voice behind him.

Decimus and Ruma were both engaged in fierce combats with their own opponents. Ruma had forced the stunned cart-driver to the ground and was raining punches on the man, who was fighting back frantically. Decimus was being held in a vicious headlock by the other robber, and was attempting to escape by repeatedly driving a fist into the man's ribcage. However, both struggles ceased abruptly when a voice pierced the silence.

'STOP FIGHTING NOW . . . OR YOUR
FRIEND DIES.'

The two combats immediately broke up;
Decimus and Ruma stepped back as the third

robber moved away from them, a blade pressed firmly under Argon's chin.

'Don't make me do anything you *boys* will regret,' said the robber. He didn't look over his shoulder, but instead shouted at the top of his voice. 'Boss? Boss! We got the upper hand h—'

There was a dull thunk, and the robber collapsed into the dirt. His sword clattered to the ground, and Argon breathed a heavy sigh of relief.

The captain of the ship was standing quite still, a mallet in his hand and a spreading smile on his lips.

Sensing the tide had turned against them, the remaining two robbers turned tail and dashed away on foot. They didn't get very far before Decimus and Ruma dragged them both back.

'Thank you, boys,' said the captain, nodding gratefully as Olu and Gladius rejoined the group. 'My name is Tonino, and I'm captain of the small boat you see moored at the jetty, there. You just saved me a *considerable* amount of money. I thank you.'

Decimus glanced briefly at the others, and stepped forward with his arm outstretched.

'Decimus Rex,' he said, greeting the captain with a firm handshake and nodding at the others. 'This is Olu, Gladius, Ruma and Argon, whose neck you just rescued. Would you like some help tying these men up? I doubt you'll get any more trouble if we secure them all to the cart ...'

The captain nodded, and together they rounded up the remaining robbers.

'Actually, we were hoping to ... hire your boat,' said Decimus, carefully. 'We need passage on quite a long journey east.'

Tonino straightened up, gazed around at the group and rubbed his chin thoughtfully.

'I have some *genuine* traders arriving in a short while,' he said, his voice edged with worry. 'If you stay with me and protect my cargo until they arrive, I promise you we'll talk about your journey east.'

He smiled hopefully at Decimus Rex, who nodded in agreement and patted the little man on the back.

'Tonino,' he said. 'We have a deal.'

COMING SOON

After a grim sea voyage, Decimus and the others find themselves in Yelang, a territory in the ancient Han Dynasty of China. Can they find Teo, the friend they thought had been killed at Suvius Tower, or are they even now walking into a deadly trap? Does Teo truly need their help, or is Slavious Doom lying in wait for them? Find out now in . . .

THE RAGING TORRENT

GLADIATOR GAME
THE SLAVEYARD HUNT

Can you find Teo's grave before the keepers catch you? This is a game for two players. Each player will secretly decide where Teo's grave is - and the other player will search for this location. Each player will have a limited number of turns in which to find it before the keepers catch up with him!

	1	2	3	4	5	6	7
A	▣		▣		▣		▣
B	▣		▣		▣		
C	▣		▣		▣	▣	▣
D		▣		▣		▣	
E		▣		▣		▣	▣
F	▣		▣			▣	
G		▣			▣		▣

HOW TO PLAY

Player 1 secretly chooses one of the graves pictured opposite and writes its grid location on a piece of paper. Player 2 does the same.

Each player then selects a character from this book by choosing a symbol below:

CHARACTERS

Decimus

Argon

Olu

Ruma

Gladius

Sturgenus

Tonino

Having chosen his character, each player takes up a pencil and, closing their eyes, jabs it (gently) into the special grid on the following pages. If the square selected contains the symbol for HIS character, he may make the number of grave searches printed next to the symbol. If it is NOT his symbol, he may only make HALF the number of searches.

Once each player knows how many searches they have, they must then take it in turns to search for Teo's grave by making a guess aloud. If one player finds the grave marked on the other player's paper, they have located Teo's resting place. If not, they are captured!

Note: the player with the fewest searches always goes first.

AN EXAMPLE

Player 1 chooses Argon (the shield symbol). He or she now jabs a pencil into the special grid on the following page and lands on Shield 4. The shield IS Argon's symbol, so player 1 may make 4 searches before his game is over.

Player 2 chooses Sturgenus (the shack symbol) and does the same. Unfortunately, he lands on Sword 6 (the symbol for Decimus), which is not his symbol, so he may only make half the number of searches (3).

The game then begins with Player 2 and they take it in turns to search the graves.

Important – if the grid is missed and the pencil hits a blank space, the player immediately gets only ONE search!

SEARCH GRID

8	6	8	6	8	4	6	2	4	4	8	8
8	4	6	2	4	4	8	8	8	4	2	6
6	4	2	2	8	4	6	2	4	4	8	8
8	4	2	6	2	8	4	6	4	2	6	2
8	6	8	6	8	4	6	2	4	4	8	8
8	4	6	2	4	4	8	8	8	4	2	6
2	8	4	6	4	2	6	2	6	4	2	2